THIS CANDLEWICK BOOK BELONGS TO:

EMMA

20 19 18 17 16 15 14 13 12 11 10 9 8 7 6 5 4 3 2 1

For Mark

Coming
ready
or
not

Copyright © 1989 by Carol Thompson

First U.S. edition 1998

Library of Congress Cataloging-in-Publication Data

Thompson, Carol.
[In my bedroom]
Piggy goes to bed / Carol Thompson. — 1st U.S. ed.
p.   cm.
Summary: A young pig's bedroom is a place
in which to play, dress, and sleep.
ISBN 0-7636-0428-3
[1. Bedrooms — Fiction. 2. Pigs — Fiction.] I. Title.
PZ7.T371423Pg   1998
[E] — dc21   97-20603

2 4 6 8 10 9 7 5 3 1

Printed in Hong Kong

This book was typeset in Esprit Book.
The pictures were done in watercolor.

Candlewick Press
2067 Massachusetts Avenue
Cambridge, Massachusetts 02140

PIGGY
GOES TO BED

ready!

Carol Thompson

CANDLEWICK PRESS
CAMBRIDGE, MASSACHUSETTS

In my bedroom I can
find all kinds of things.

a bed

a chair   a toy box

The toy box is full of things
to play with.

a duck

a train

some blocks

a hat

My chair can be
anything.

a lookout post

something to drive

a secret place

I can even sit on it!

I keep my clothes in a special place.

There is a bar to hang things from
and there are shoes on the floor.

It makes a good hiding place.

The shelves are for my favorite things.

a piggy bank

books

all my crayons
for drawing

My bed is just right
for me.

It has a pillow,   a light beside it,

a potty underneath,   and a soft blanket.

I dress in my bedtime
clothes.

pajamas

slippers

a bathrobe
with a tie

When I go to bed

I take my best friend with me.

CAROL THOMPSON is the author-illustrator of *Piggy Washes Up* and the illustrator of *Bumpety Bump* and *Bounce Bounce Bounce,* by Kathy Henderson, and *Oops-A-Daisy!,* by Joyce Dunbar. She has won numerous awards for her work as a fabric designer.